This book belongs to

_____

_____

MARY ENGELBREIT'S
MOTHER GOOSE

FAVORITES

HARPERCOLLINS*PUBLISHERS*

Humpty Dumpty sat on a wall,
Humpty Dumpty had a great fall.
All the king's horses
And all the king's men
Couldn't put Humpty Dumpty together again.

Baa, baa, black sheep, have you any wool?

Yes, sir, yes, sir, three bags full.

One for my master, one for my dame,

And one for the little boy who lives down the lane.

This little piggie went to market,

This little piggie stayed at home,

This little piggie had roast beef,

This little piggie had none,

And this little piggie cried,

Wee-wee-wee-wee-wee,

All the way home.

ittle Miss Muffet
  Sat on a tuffet,
Eating her curds and whey;
Along came a spider,
Who sat down beside her
And frightened Miss Muffet away.

Pat-a-cake, pat-a-cake, baker's man!
Bake me a cake as fast as you can.
Roll it, and pat it, and mark it with B,
Put it in the oven for Baby and me.

The Queen
of Hearts,
She made
some tarts,
All on a
summer's day;
The Knave of Hearts,
He stole those tarts,
And took them
clean away.

The King of Hearts
Called for the tarts
And beat the knave full sore;
The Knave of Hearts
Brought back the tarts
And vowed he'd steal no more.

Old King Cole was a merry old soul
And a merry old soul was he;
He called for his pipe,
And he called for his bowl,
And he called for his fiddlers three.

Every fiddler, he had a fine fiddle,
And a very fine fiddle had he;
Oh, there's none so rare
As can compare
With King Cole
And his fiddlers three.

Three little ghostesses,
Sitting on postesses,
Eating buttered toastesses,
Greasing their fistesses,
Up to their wristesses,
Oh, what beastesses
To make such feastesses!

Hickory, dickory, dock,
The mouse ran up the clock.
The clock struck one,
The mouse ran down,
Hickory, dickory, dock.

ack and Jill went up the hill
To fetch a pail of water;
Jack fell down and broke his crown,
And Jill came tumbling after.

Then up Jack got and off did trot,
As fast as he could caper,
To old Dame Dob, who patched his nob,
With vinegar and brown paper.

There was a crooked man
Who walked a crooked mile.
He found a crooked sixpence
Against a crooked stile;
He bought a crooked cat,
Which caught a crooked mouse,
And they all lived together
In a little crooked house.

Pease porridge hot,
Pease porridge cold,
Pease porridge in the pot,
Nine days old.
Some like it hot,
Some like it cold,
Some like it in the pot,
Nine days old.

here was a little girl,
And she had a little curl
Right in the middle
Of her forehead;
When she was good
She was very very good,
But when she was bad
She was horrid.

Little boy blue,
    Come blow your horn,
        The sheep's in the meadow,
        The cow's in the corn.
        Where is the boy
            Who looks after the sheep?
            He's under a haystack
            Fast asleep.

Little Bo-Peep has lost her sheep
And can't tell where to find them;
Leave them alone, and they'll come home,
Wagging their tails behind them.

The three little kittens
They lost their mittens,
And they began to cry,

Oh, Mother dear,
We sadly fear
Our mittens we have lost.

What? Lost your mittens,
You naughty kittens!
Then you shall have no pie.

Mee-ow, mee-ow, mee-ow.

No, you shall have no pie.

The three little kittens
They found their mittens,
And they began to cry,

Oh, Mother dear,
See here, see here,
Our mittens we have found.

Put on your mittens,
You silly kittens,
And you shall have some pie.

Purr-r, purr-r, purr-r,
Oh, let us have some pie.

Rub-a-dub-dub, three men in a tub,
And who do you think they be?
The butcher, the baker,
The candlestick-maker,
Turn them out, knaves all three.

Row, row, row your boat
Gently down the stream.
Merrily, merrily, merrily, merrily,
Life is but a dream.

ey diddle, diddle,
The Cat and the Fiddle,
The Cow jumped over the Moon,
The little Dog laughed
To see such sport,
And the Dish ran away
With the Spoon.

Star light, star bright,
First star I see tonight,
I wish I may, I wish I might,
Have the wish I wish tonight.

I see the moon,
And the moon sees me,
God bless the moon,
And God bless me.

Twinkle, twinkle, little star,
How I wonder what you are!
Up above the world so high,
Like a diamond in the sky.

29

ee Willie Winkie
Runs through the town,
Upstairs and downstairs
In his nightgown,
Rapping at the window,
Crying through the lock,
Are the children in their beds,
For now it's eight o'clock?

Mary Engelbreit's Mother Goose Favorites
Collection copyright © 2008 by Mary Engelbreit Ink
Illustrations copyright © 2005 by Mary Engelbreit Ink

Manufactured in Mexico
ISBN 978-0-06-157544-0

Typography by Stephanie Bart-Horvath
❖